THE FAMOUS FIVE
SHORT STORIES

WELL DONE, FAMOUS FIVE

D1353104

The Famous Five

Timmy   Anne   Dick   Julian   George

Text copyright © Enid Blyton, 1956
Illustrations copyright © Jamie Littler, 2014

Enid Blyton's signature is a registered trade mark of Hodder & Stoughton Ltd

Text first published in Great Britain in Enid Blyton's Magazine Annual – No. 3, in 1956.
Also available in The Famous Five Short Stories, published by Hodder Children's Books.
First published in Great Britain in this edition in 2014 by Hodder Children's Books

The rights of Enid Blyton and Jamie Littler to be identified as the Author
and Illustrator of the Work respectively have been asserted by them in
accordance with the Copyright, Designs and Patents Act 1988

2

A Catalogue record for this book is available from the British Library
ISBN 978 1 444 91632 4

Printed in China
Hodder Children's Books
A division of Hachette Children's Books
Hachette UK Limited, 338 Euston Road, London NW1 3BH

www.hachette.co.uk

Enid Blyton

WELL DONE, FAMOUS FIVE

illustrated by **Jamie Littler**

h
Hodder
Children's
Books

A division of Hachette Children's Books

Famous Five Colour Reads

For a complete list of the full-length
Famous Five adventures, turn to
the last page of this book

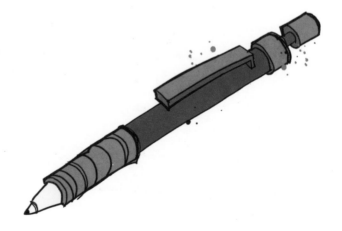

Contents

CHAPTER ONE

'Nice to be together again,' said Julian.
'All Five of us!'

George nodded. 'Yes, Timmy's thrilled too. Aren't you, Tim?'

Timmy the dog barked, and laid his big head on George's knee, and she patted him.

All **the Five** were on the top of **Kirrin Hill,** looking at the wide spread of country stretched out below them. Anne was handing out the picnic food, and Dick passed it round.

Timmy raised his head
at once, and sniffed. *Would
there be anything for him?*

'Of course, Timmy,' said Anne. **'A bone –**
and **two big dog biscuits.'**

10

'As well as a good part of our own sandwiches and buns, I expect,' said Dick. **'No, Tim** – that pile's mine – and I'm **not** going to exchange my biscuits for yours!'

'What a **wonderful view** we've got from here,' said Julian, beginning to munch his sandwich. 'We can see for **miles and miles** all round us.'

'Well – not much is happening,' said Anne, 'except that those sheep are rambling around that field, and those cows are doing what they always do – eat, eat, eat all day long – although if I had to eat nothing but grass, I'd soon stop!'

'Can't see a soul about,' said Dick, lazily. 'I suppose it's everyone's dinner-time.

Now, **why can't something exciting happen,** just to give us a bit of interest while we're eating! We've had so many adventures that I'm beginning to feel quite cheated if one doesn't turn up as soon as **we're together again!'**

CHAPTER TWO.

'Oh, for goodness' sake, **don't wish for an adventure today!'**

said Anne. 'I like a bit of peace. I don't want to choke with excitement when I'm eating these **delicious sandwiches!** What has Aunt Fan put into them?'

'A bit of everything in the
larder, I should think,' said George.

‘Get away, Tim – don’t breathe **all over me** like that!’

'What's that moving right away over there – along the side of that hill?' asked Dick, suddenly. 'Is it cows?'

Everyone looked. 'Too far away to see,' said George. 'Can't be cows, though – they don't move like cows – cows walk so slowly.'

'Well, they must be **horses** then,' said Julian.

'But who'd have so many horses out for exercise round here?' said George. 'All the horses are farm horses – they'd be working in the fields, not trotting in a row across a hillside.'

'It must be a riding school, idiot,' said Dick. 'If we had **our binoculars,** we'd see a lot of nicely behaved little girls from some nearby school cantering along on their nicely behaved horses!'

'I did bring my binoculars – didn't you notice?'

said George, rummaging about behind her.

'I put them down here somewhere – ah,
here they are. Want them, Dick?'

Dick took them and put them to his eyes. **'Yes** – **it's a line of horses** – about six – wonderful ones, too. But it's not girls who are riding them – it's boys – stable boys, I think.'

'Oh, of course – I forgot,' said George. 'They're wonderful **racing horses** from **Lord Daniron's stable** – they have to be **exercised each day.**

'Can you see a **very big horse** in the line, Dick? A magnificent creature – he's called

Thunder-Along,

and he's the **most valuable horse** in the **country** – so they say!'

CHAPTER THREE

Dick was now examining the horses with much interest, holding the binoculars to his eyes.

'They're lovely horses – and yes, I think I can see the one you mean, George. A great horse with a wonderful head – he's the first one of all.'

'Let me see,' said George.

Dick held on to the binoculars. 'No. Half a mo. Hey – **something's happening!'**

'What is it?' said George.

Dick added, 'Something seemed to **rush** straight across **in front** of **Thunder-Along** – was it a fox or a dog? Oh, he's **rearing up** in **fright,** he's in **quite a panic.**

He . . .' Then Dick suddenly shouted, **'HE'S OFF!**

He's **thrown** his groom – yes, he's on the ground, **hurt,** I think – and **HE'S BOLTING!** Oh no – **HE'LL KILL HIMSELF.'**

A silence fell on the Five. Even Timmy was quiet, staring in the same direction as the others. George made as if to snatch her binoculars away from Dick, but he dodged, gluing them to his eyes.

'Don't lose sight of the horse, Dick, **keep the binoculars on him,**' said Julian, urgently. 'He's the finest horse this country has. **Watch him – watch where he goes!** We may be the only people who can see the way he takes.'

He's still bolting at **top speed** –

I hope he doesn't **run into a tree** –

'No, he *just* missed that one.

Oh, now he's come to a gate –

a **HIGH GATE . . .**'

CHAPTER FOUR

The others had now lost sight of the horse and were hanging on to **every word of Dick's.**

Timmy was so excited that he began to bark, sensing the general excitement. George shushed him, fearing to lose something that Dick said.

'He's over the gate – what a jump, oh what a jump! Now he's **galloping** down **the road** – I can't see him – **yes,** there he is again – he's come to **the stream** – **he's over it,**

cleared it beautifully – away he goes, **up Rilling Hill** – now he's going more slowly – he must be absolutely puffed. **He's gone** into a **field of corn** – the farmer won't like that!' said Dick.

He continued, 'And now – he must be **lying down** in the corn! **I can't see him any more!'**

George snatched the binoculars from Dick – no, she couldn't see him either.

She switched them to **the hillside** where the horses had been exercising.

What a **commotion!** The grooms were talking excitedly, pointing here and there, evidently at a loss to know where **Thunder-Along** had **gone!**

CHAPTER FIVE

'I'm afraid this is **the end** of **our picnic,'** said Julian. 'As long as Thunder-Along is in the field of corn, resting, he's safe – but if he goes off again, **anything may happen!'**

He added, 'We've got to **report our news at once** – and Dick, you'd better **bike** as **fast** as you can to that **cornfield.** Maybe the horse will still be there.'

Dick ran to where he had left his bike, and leapt on it.

The others went to theirs, too, and soon
they were riding off to **Kirrin** to report their
news to **the police,** who would at once get in
touch with **the stables.**

Dick planned out his way as he went. What would be the best way to get quickly to Rilling Hill? He soon made up his mind, and **cycled along at top speed.** It seemed a very long way – but at last he was cycling **up the hill** to where he hoped to find the field of corn. He was so OUT OF BREATH that he had to **get off his bike** and **walk.**

He came to the field-gate and looked in cautiously at the corn. He could see **no horse at all** – and no wonder, for he would be **lying down!**

'I'll have to tread in carefully,' thought Dick. 'I can see the way he trod – where the corn's flattened.' So in he went – only to hear a furious voice yelling at him from the gate behind him.

'Come out of that **corn!**
Come out at once!' It was the
farmer, red with anger. Dick didn't like to yell
back, in case he frightened the horse.

So he **pointed urgently** into the **field** and went carefully on.
 'You wait!' yelled the farmer. 'I'll get **the police** on to you!'

CHAPTER SIX

Suddenly Dick **saw the horse.** It lay
in the corn, ears pricked up, **eyes rolling.**

Dick stopped. 'Well, old beauty?' he said. 'Well, you **magnificent thing! Thunder-Along!** Do you know

your name? Poor boy, **how frightened you were!** Come now, **come! You're safe** – come along with me!'

To his surprise and delight the great
horse stood up and flicked his ears to and fro,
watching Dick carefully. Then he whinnied
a little, and stepped towards him.

The boy took hold of the reins gently,
and dared to rub the velvety nose.

Then he led the horse
carefully out of the corn.

The farmer stood staring in amazement at the magnificent creature.

'But – but, isn't that Lord Daniron's horse, Thunder-Along?' he said, almost in a whisper. 'Did he bolt?'

Dick nodded his head. 'Keep my bike for me, will you?' he said. **'I must** take the horse while **he's quiet.** I expect as

soon as the owners know where he is, they'll **send a horsebox.** I'll lead him up and down the lane for a little, till they come.'

CHAPTER SEVEN

It wasn't long before a **great horsebox** drove slowly up the lane, and **Thunder-Along's own groom** came to pet him and lead him quietly into it.

He ran his
eyes over the
horse carefully.

'No damage done!' he said.
'Thank goodness you had
binoculars with you, boy, and
saw where he went. You did well
to get him!'

As soon as the horsebox had gone down the hill, **Dick** **jumped** **on his** **bike** and rode away.

He soon met the others, cycling towards him, anxious to know what had happened. Timmy was running beside them.

'The **horse** was **all right. I** got him, and there's **not a scratch on him!'** said Dick. 'What a bit of luck we had this morning, **looking** through **your binoculars,** George! What do you say, Timmy?'

'**Woof!'** said Timmy, agreeing as usual, '**Woof!'**

'He says it's the kind of thing that would happen to **the Famous Five!**' said George. And, of course, **she was quite right!**

If you enjoyed this Famous Five short story, there's plenty more action and adventure in the full-length Famous Five novels. Here is a list of all the titles, in the order they were first published.